MASTERS of DISASTER

MASTERS
of
DISASTER

GARY PAULSEN

WENDY
LAMB
BOOKS

Copyright © 2010 by Gary Paulsen
All rights reserved. Published in the United States by Wendy Lamb Books,
an imprint of Random House Children's Books, a division of Random House,
Inc., New York.

Wendy Lamb Books and the colophon are trademarks of Random House, Inc.

Three chapters in this work are based upon stories by Gary Paulsen previously
published in *Boys' Life* magazine: "Henry Mosley's Last Stand" (July 2001),
"Breaking the Record" (March 2003), and "The Night the Headless, Blood-
Drinking, Flesh-Eating Corpses of Cleveland (Almost) Took Over the World"
(July 2004).

Visit us on the Web! www.randomhouse.com/kids
Educators and librarians, for a variety of teaching tools, visit us at
www.randomhouse.com/teachers

Library of Congress Cataloging-in-Publication Data is available upon request.
ISBN: 978-0-385-73997-9 (trade)   ISBN: 978-0-385-90816-0 (lib. bdg.)
ISBN: 978-0-375-89867-9 (ebook)

Printed in the United States of America
10 9 8 7 6 5 4 3 2 1
First Edition

This book is dedicated to my dear friend
Craig Virden;
always a wonderful boy at heart
who knew the joy of bringing books to boys
and boys to books.

MASTERS
of
DISASTER

1

The Launch of a Grand Plan

"I've called you here today, men, because I have an important announcement. One that will change our lives."

Henry Mosley licked his finger and carefully flipped a page of densely scribbled notes on the yellow legal pad in front of him. He cleared his throat, looked up and made eye contact with his audience.

Henry's audience was small—just Reed Hamner and Riley Dolen, his best friends—and they were sitting at his kitchen table after school, but still, he knew that every good public speaker, not to mention every effective leader, understood the significance of Looking a Man in the Eye.

Henry Mosley was twelve years old. He had recently watched a documentary about General Douglas MacArthur with his grandfather, an army veteran, during which he had been very impressed with Military Precision and Choosing Words Carefully, not to mention Examples of Bravery and Inventiveness.

Earlier, at school, Henry had told Reed and Riley that he needed to speak with them regarding a Subject of the Utmost Importance and that they should meet at his house at precisely 1600 hours.

Reed had been late, of course, because it took him a while to figure out what 1600 hours was, and he was always late because he got lost a lot, even though he only lived three streets over. Riley had not only been on time, but he had also brought granola bars and Ziploc bags of fresh vegetables and bottles of water for all three of them because he knew that meetings required snacks, and Riley was always prepared. Always.

"I am proposing," Henry continued, reading carefully from his notes, "that we Undertake and Implement a Series of Daring Experiences and

Grand Adventures the likes of which the history of Western civilization has never seen, at least not from twelve-year-olds in suburban Cleveland."

Reed scratched his ear and looked confused. Reed frequently looked confused. Riley snapped a carrot stick in half and looked thoughtful—his usual expression.

"Why?" Reed finally asked, a hint of panic in his voice. "Why are we underwhatsitting and imple-whoositting?"

"Henry's got spring fever," Riley explained, somewhat dismissively, Henry thought.

"What I have in mind is so much bigger than that," Henry said. "I'm working to create a series of tasks that will Prove Our Manhood and show us What We're Made Of. And if we play our cards right, we just might Alter the Course of History a time or two. And, of course, Impress Girls and Get Them to Notice Us."

"What made you start thinking about things like experiences and adventures and bravery and what we're made of?" Reed was chewing a fingernail and looking as if he had to go to the bathroom. Urgently.

"English class."

"What happened during fifth period?" Riley asked. "And what got you talking so official-like and, I dunno, *epic?*" Henry had a way of always sounding like whatever he was currently reading or watching, and Riley racked his brains to remember whether their reading list lately had included any books about military history or Greek mythology.

"Remember how we read *Huckleberry Finn* and *Treasure Island* and the book about how the kids tried to save their father from the space-time continuum thingie and that other book about the boy who got stuck in the woods after a plane crash? I got to thinking—what would *our* stories be like? What would an author write about us? Let's face facts: We may be the most boring twelve-year olds on the planet."

"We're not boring, Henry," Reed said in a small voice.

"Really? Because I've been thinking about our lives lately and perfect attendance does not count as exciting."

"Well, we don't just go to school, we also, um, we, ah, well, there's . . . and then, of course, er . . ." Reed looked to Riley for help, but Riley just shrugged.

4

"Exactly," Henry said. "Nothing interesting ever happens. Luckily, I have plenty of ideas."

"What kind of ideas?"

"You leave the details to me." Henry patted his legal pad confidently.

"Does that mean you're in charge? Like the boss or something?" Reed always cared about who was in charge. He was the only boy in his family—he had three older sisters and three younger sisters—and he never got his way at home. Never. Not ever.

"Of course not. This is a democracy; we vote on everything."

"Then I vote no. I don't want to complain or worry anyone, but adventures sound dangerous. And I have a curfew. I don't have time to change history if I have to be in the house by eight o'clock on weekdays. Or whatever the new way of saying eight o'clock is."

"The voting starts later, when I tell you each plan. The idea to go ahead with Becoming Men of Action and Daring, Masters of Adventure, well, I've already made *that* executive decision for all of us."

"Like I said, my curfew is eight on school nights and that's only if I've gotten my homework done.

And doesn't *daring* usually mean *painful*? I don't like pain."

"There might be some pain," Henry allowed, "but not much. Probably. Hardly any. Maybe a little, but no blood. Definitely no blood. Well, okay, maybe a smidge, but not enough to worry about." To Reed, Henry sounded as if he'd be disappointed if there weren't pain and blood.

"What do you think?" Reed looked at Riley, who had been taking notes. Riley's mother was a reporter and his father was a court stenographer, so Reed and Henry were used to seeing Riley quietly scribbling in a notebook, not only in class, but during routine conversations. Riley's attention to detail had resolved more than a few arguments over the years when they went back and consulted his jottings. He wasn't a big talker like Henry and he wasn't a nervous babbler like Reed. He took notes.

"I want to see what happens," Riley said now, looking up from his notebook. "I'm in."

"See? Even without a formal vote, majority rules," Henry said, smiling.

Reed put his head between his knees and tried to breathe slowly because he'd heard that this technique made your heart stop racing and helped the swirly blobs in front of your eyes go away. The upside-down position only made his ears ring more loudly.

"I'm going to tweak the ideas for a few more days," Henry said to the top of Reed's head, "and we'll reconvene this weekend and get started."

"Reconvene?" Reed asked. "You mean meet up?"

"Don't worry, Reed," Riley said. "I know a website where you can draw up your last will and testament." Although he was only twelve, Riley had already written several drafts of his own will. He liked to be prepared.

"See how interesting things have gotten already?" Henry asked. "Did you think when you got up in the morning that you'd be writing a will in the afternoon? My plan is revving things up around here."

"I'm not sure I'm the kind of person who was meant for an interesting life," Reed said, raising his head. "I think my Inner Courageous Guy might be hibernating. Or nonexistent."

"That's exactly why we need to start doing Interesting Things That Will Build Our Character," Henry said. "Otherwise we could wind up like Dwight Hauser."

Reed and Riley both frowned. At their school, Dwight Hauser was just another way of saying "stuck-up, pushy jerk," "puke-spewing slimeball" or "nose-picking, booger-eating punk." Dwight Hauser was an out-and-out bully, but Henry, Riley and Reed knew that he was yellow clear through, because he only picked on girls or younger kids. Hauser was always surrounded by a rumor-spreading group of tiny-minded toadies who had been scheming for years to slip iguana poop into the beef stew in the lunchroom.

"Well, if you put it like that," Reed said, "I'll keep you guys company. If you insist."

"You wait and see," Henry said. "You're going to wind up thanking me for coming up with this Plan of Action. I have a feeling, men, that it's going to be the best thing that ever happened to us."

2

Breaking the Record

"I have it: the absolutely perfect first idea."

Henry held up a yellow legal pad covered with calculations. He was sitting next to Reed and Riley on his back steps the following Saturday morning. They'd met at 0900 hours, which wasn't too tricky for Reed to figure out, but he was still late because he'd overslept and then he'd taken a right when he meant to take a left at the Petersons' house on the corner because Erika Peterson was getting in the car to go to figure-skating lessons and Reed thought Erika was so pretty he had a hard time telling right from left when he saw her.

Riley, of course, had been early and had brought a three-ring binder full of loose-leaf paper, a small digital voice recorder with extra batteries, a new box of mechanical pencils, and a morning snack of three oranges, because he believed in being prepared. For any eventuality. Always.

"Perfect idea for what?" Reed's voice was shaking and he wiped his sweaty hands on his jeans.

"Our first adventure. Men, we're ready to begin."

"You sound so sure. But how do you know?" Reed's voice cracked. "I'm not at all sure we're anywhere near ready. I mean, you know, *ready* is such a big word. Maybe you should tell us what you're thinking about first and then we can talk about it for a while, a really long while, because it might take us a long time to get ready. If, you know, we ever are."

Henry waved the legal pad, which was covered with sketches and formulas and diagrams and notes and printouts from Web articles as if he were swatting away Reed's worries like flies.

"We have to do something that breaks a record." He paused dramatically. Henry jotted a few more notes while Reed stared off into space, thinking of how much he loved his family, even his third-littlest sister, and how much he would miss them, kind of, when one of Henry's record-breaking plans got him killed. Because breaking records went hand in hand with the possibility of death—no one ever broke records by sitting quietly or petting the cat. Breaking records usually had to do with speed and sometimes sharp objects or explosive devices and paramedics standing by with a defibrillator and fire extinguishers.

Riley pondered Henry's announcement. "Do you mean a city record? Or county? Or state?"

Henry shook his head. "World record. Otherwise nobody will pay any attention."

"Of course." Riley underlined *world* in his notes.

"I've given it a lot of thought." Henry flipped to the second page of his legal pad. "The hardest part was deciding just what record to break, or make, since some of the ones I thought about have never been done. There's no current record for kids staying alive underwater. Weird, huh? And I was bummed to find out that there's, um, what's it called?"—he consulted his pad—"an 'ethics regulation' against getting a white rat drunk and then teaching him to drive a model car in order to do a study of drunk driving—something about cruelty to animals, even though I'd have put a tiny seat belt on the rat. And my research about making a capsule and riding in an oil pipeline from one pumping station to the next, you know, to see what it's like to be oil, didn't work out. Everyone I called hung up on me."

"Living underwater? Driving rats? Oil?" Reed muttered numbly as he watched Riley list the possible records in neat columns.

"Since this is our first try," Henry continued, "I figure we need to start with resources we can easily find and a situation that's at least kind of familiar. The perfect solution, obviously, is bikes." He jumped up to face them. "We are going to break the world record for the most forward airborne somersaults on a bike."

Silence.

"Exactly," Henry said. "It's perfect. I knew you'd agree."

At last Reed said, "I've watched those extreme bike competitions on TV. Those guys are amazing, doing backflips and twists and off-the-bike somersaults—two, sometimes two and a half or even three complete rolls with a full doppelganger and a whizbanger or whatever they call them. What's so special and record-breaking about forward somersaults?"

"Here's how I see it," Henry said. "Nobody, especially not a guy our age, has even done one forward somersault, blindfolded, with their hands tied together and then to the handlebars. I'm sure it's never been done. So even if we get *one*, we've got the record. And if we get *four* . . . well, that's just the Most Awesome Thing Ever."

Riley looked up from his notes. "Henry, somebody will have to get pretty high to make four somersaults with a bicycle tied to his hands."

"Forty-seven feet," Henry said. "I worked it out with a calculator."

"Oh, well, if it's just that . . . ," Reed said. "I thought it was going to be hard." He started laughing, then stopped when Henry and Riley didn't join in. "Wait—you guys aren't seriously considering that, are you?"

Henry went on, "The hard part is going to be when you—"

"You who? Who is *you?*" Reed sounded like an owl. "Who? Who?"

"Who does this, you mean? Well, obviously, I'd

like to, but I was the one who came up with the idea and I've done all the calculations and I'll be point man during the jump, busy measuring and organizing and double-checking every safety detail. So it can't be me."

Reed turned hopefully to Riley, who pointed to his notebook. "My talents are best suited to recording the event for posterity."

"Posterity," Reed said with a resigned sigh, "sounds like a fancy way of saying 'watching Reed get his butt kicked and his guts hung up on tree limbs approximately forty-seven feet off the ground.'"

"Maybe," Riley said. "Depending on luck."

"Nah," Henry said. "Look at it this way: You were the least jazzed about the whole thing, so it'll be that much more amazing if you're the one to do the first adventure. Plus, it'll be your name in the record books because you'll be the record-breaker, the one everyone remembers."

"Oh, well, when you put it that way . . ." Reed didn't sound convinced.

Henry rubbed his hands together. "Good! Let's get going; we're wasting daylight."

"Today? Wh-wh-why s-s-so s-s-suddenly?" Reed's right eye twitched and his teeth chattered.

Henry and Riley looked at each other. They ignored Reed's panic attack. They pulled him to his feet and started walking to his house to pick up his bicycle. Henry dragged a red wagon loaded with boxes as he debated with Riley about angles and height differentials and the virtue of measurements in feet versus meters. Reed staggered along in a fog of terror.

Henry said, "I know the perfect place to do this."

Reed went into his garage and got his bike.

"The Batsons' house." Henry nodded. "They're away on vacation and my sister Lauren is feeding their guinea pigs and watering the plants. I borrowed their house key so we can get into the attic. They have a steeply pitched roof, which makes for the perfect angle sloping down to the backyard." He started toward the Batsons'.

"*Roof?*" Reed hadn't quite caught up. "You want me to ride off a *roof?*"

"Of course. The distance from the roof to the ground will allow for the number of rotations we require. And we can't underestimate the value of privacy—no one will disturb us or rip off our idea. Plus, and this is key, the Batsons are the only family in town with a Hydro 3000 super-reinforced, spring-loaded cover on their swimming pool."

"Wh-wh-wh-why d-d-d-does th-th-that m-m-m-matter?" Reed's teeth started chattering again.

"For altitude, in case you miss the diving board and, of course, as a safety net after you complete the stunt," Henry said, shaking his head. "Isn't that obvious? The additional bounce from the springs should assist you to do additional forward somersaults in midair before you come to rest. Who knows? You might even get six or seven."

"Is that legal?" Riley asked. "I'm pretty sure records are only valid if you follow all the rules. Otherwise the whole thing could wind up being for nothing."

"I looked up the regulations on the extreme bike website and there's nothing about springboards being prohibited. You just can't use a motor. Which was good to know even though it ruined my plan to attach an old Corvette engine to the bike and add speed to the equation."

"You want me to drive off the roof of a house

and bounce on a diving board with a bicycle?" Reed had stopped walking. "That's what you're after here?"

"Of course," Henry said, "because just riding off the roof would be stupid. You start at the highest point of the roof, shoot down the incline, touch-and-go on the diving board and do the flips over the pool so that you eventually land on the cover, which is top-of-the-line and has the necessary, um"—he glanced down at his legal pad—"tensile strength to support your weight."

Riley looked up from his own set of notes. "Do the Batsons know we're diving off their roof, bouncing a kid and a bike on their diving board and landing on their pool cover?"

Henry shrugged. "Not really. I thought it best to keep our plans private."

"Good thinking."

"Wait a minute." Reed shook his head as Henry's idea continued to slowly sink in. "Are we absolutely positive that driving a bike off a roof is the best way to break a record?"

"Yep, off that roof." Henry pointed at the Batsons' house and nodded approvingly. The house was three stories high with a sharply peaked roof and reminded Reed of a castle. An ugly old castle where bad things happened to boys who let themselves get talked into doing stupid things just to get their stupid name in a stupid record book.

Henry pulled the key out of his pocket and led Reed and Riley to the back door. Reed's knees were trembling so hard that Henry and Riley had to carry his bike up the stairs while he remained glued to the kitchen floor. They left the bike near the window in the attic and jogged back downstairs to pry Reed's hands off the back door. While Henry pushed and Riley pulled the rigid Reed up the stairs, Henry chatted encouragingly to Reed. "C'mon, open your eyes. Just one more flight. You can do this. Let go of the railing. Look—almost there. It's going to be a piece of cake, you'll see. I can't feel my arm because you're holding on so tight you're cutting off the circulation. It'll be over so fast you'll want to do it again. Trust me, buddy."

It took some convincing to keep Reed moving, but there was no need to use a tranquilizer gun and throw him over their shoulders (even though Henry had that option in his plans, just in case). They finally got Reed up to the Batsons' roof and shoved him out the window. Riley stood next to him, holding a handful of Reed's shirt so he wouldn't make a run for it or fall, while Henry ran downstairs and carried the boxes from the red wagon upstairs.

Reed refused to open his eyes, much less help, so Henry and Riley had to dress him. Henry had raided his garage of every piece of athletic protection his father, a PE instructor, had collected over the years. They forced the football pads over Reed's head and tied the laces snug across his chest. Henry wedged a mouth guard between Reed's clenched teeth as Riley strapped soccer shin pads on Reed's lower legs. They threw a quick game of scissors/paper/rock to figure out who had to shove the cup down the front of Reed's football pants.

After Henry and Riley had dressed Reed in all the protective gear they had, they sat him on his bike, slapped a hockey goalie's helmet on and adjusted the band on the goggles. Reed started to scream when Henry tried to tie the bandana around his eyes, so, sadly, they decided against adding the blindfold to the stunt. It was okay, though, Henry figured, because Reed had his eyes shut tight. Riley, who had a first-aid kit poking out of his backpack because he believed in always being prepared, began wrapping Reed's hands to the handlebars with an Ace bandage.

"Let's do this!" Henry slapped Reed's back.

"No. I really don't want to. You know, all things considered. It's a whole lot of altitude."

"Reed," Riley said. "You're forgetting it will be your name in the record book. *You're* the one who will be famous. *You're* the one who'll have all the girls thinking you're really cool."

"Well, when you put it that way . . . But still, it's a heck of a long way down and I think—"

"*Go!*" Henry shoved Reed from behind.

The bike tottered from the impact, and for a second, Henry thought Reed would skid down the roof on his side, thereby ruining the entire project. But Reed's instincts for self-preservation kicked in—he regained his balance and righted the bike as momentum took over and he began hurtling down the roof.

Riley noted the time and wrote it down.

At the instant Reed hit the bottom edge of the roof he was moving at something approaching terminal velocity, which Henry had researched and discovered was about 120 miles an hour for a falling body. The bearings on the bike were nearly smoking.

At this point, Henry was glad he'd abandoned the idea of shaving Reed's head and greasing it with petroleum jelly to reduce friction. It probably wouldn't have increased the speed much, and Reed would have objected more. Henry glanced down at his list and made an X through VASELINE ON BALD HEAD.

Reed flew off the roof and seemed to hover in midair for an astonishingly long time, even though Riley only counted to two-Mississippi in his head. Reed's eyes were still screwed shut, so he didn't see Henry grinning and flashing him a thumbs-up, or Riley, who was wishing he'd brought his video camera.

"Noooooooooooooooooooooo!" Reed howled as he dropped out of sight.

Five Mississippies later, as Henry and Riley were scrambling to the edge of the roof to look down over the yard, Reed reappeared in front of them, much higher than the edge of the roof.

Amazingly, Reed had hit the diving board perfectly in the center, and the force of the impact had snap-propelled him and the bike back up in the air. ("About," Riley wrote later in his project summary, "like someone flicking a booger off a finger.")

Reed dropped like a stone before Henry or Riley could say anything, and they saw him plummet toward the ground for the second time. This time they heard the scream as he dropped: *"Call 9-1-1!"*

Although the first landing was picture perfect, on the next bounce Reed was leaning slightly to his left and the bike shot out sideways due to the force and angle of the impact. He'd have fallen off the bike if not for the Ace bandage binding him to the handlebars. The bike skidded on the diving board and ricocheted off at a forty-five-degree angle, aiming Reed at the back alley. The speed was more than Henry had ever hoped for.

Reed flew headfirst into a collection of plastic garbage cans, dragging the bike behind him, crashing through two trash bags full of used disposable diapers.

Which didn't slow him down at all.

Reed seemed to pick up speed as he hit almost everything else along the side of the Batsons' alley for the next half block. He hammered two more garbage cans, avoided mowing down Mrs. Hooperman's cockapoo by a good four and a half inches, and after a carom off the Kleins' garage, exploded into a classic parabolic projectile curve, during which he did one full and complete, perfect forward somersault, before coming to rest sitting against a rusted-out Chevy half-ton truck, a disposable diaper covering his head and face.

In a voice muffled by the diaper and its contents, most of which was oozing down his neck, he called out to Henry and Riley: "Man, that would have been soooo bad without a helmet."

"You know, Riley, I don't think the extreme bike people are going to acknowledge the record without objective witnesses or some kind of photograph or video proof," Henry said as they climbed back up the roof to the window. "Video! I should have thought of that before Reed took off on the bike. Plus, we'd have to be able to prove the actual height Reed achieved, even though I'm dead certain it was way over the forty-seven feet I estimated."

"Don't feel bad, Henry," Riley said. "Look at this as a test run for future events—now we know we need cameras to document and authenticate what we do. But I bet we can get the plans for the house at the county assessor's office and determine the exact height of the roof anyway."

"I think," Henry mused aloud as they headed

down the stairs and out the back door, "that given the height of the first bounce and even allowing for the fact that the back tire slipped the second time, torquing the landing, and despite the fact that we can't prove we broke a record, the project was a complete success."

"Yep," Riley answered as he cut the Ace bandage and released Reed from the bike.

They pulled Reed away from the scattered garbage.

"Amazing, man, you were brilliant," Henry said.

"Bad break to have nailed those diapers, buddy," Riley said to Reed. Then he turned to Henry. "I'm going to need your plans, Henry, for my report."

"Sure thing." Henry nodded. "Let's hose Reed off—I forgot that the Batsons have a new baby—and go get something to eat. I'm starving."

"How'd I do?" Reed asked. Even though his hands had been freed, he made no move to take the diaper off his face. "Did we get the record? It felt like we got the record. I mean, it's all a blur, and while I don't mean to complain, I can't see anything, and I was just wondering if that was a side effect of the altitude, like when you get dizzy when you go skiing in Colorado."

24

Henry gently pulled the diaper off Reed's head. "Yeah, Reed, you shattered that record all over the place. Good job, buddy. You were beyond awesome—that was the coolest thing I've ever seen, and you handled the whole thing like a professional stuntman or daredevil. Seems like maybe you were born for adventure."

"You know, that's exactly what I was thinking. Right after my life flashed before my eyes and just before everything started smelling like doody. Why does everything smell like doody?" Reed looked at their leader.

"That," Henry said, "is the smell of victory. The Wonderful Smell of Victory."

3

Wildlife in the Woods

"All right, men, here's the next plan." Henry reached into his locker after third period and pulled out a yellow legal pad. He cleared his throat and started reading to Reed and Riley.

"Because it's Friday, we head for the bush directly after school this afternoon and we don't come back until Sunday—two days living by our wits. We don't bring anything but the clothes we're wearing—no food, no matches, no shelter: nothing. I found the perfect spot on the map, it's in the woods by where the railroad bridge crosses the river. It's totally deserted."

"Today? Like in four hours when school gets out?" Reed, who had been leaning against the wall, slipped to a sitting position on the floor.

Henry nodded. "Spontaneity. Adds excitement to the event."

Reed shook his head. "I still smell doody from the bike jump last week. It's like it's in my pores."

"Maybe you still smell it, but you don't reek— that fifteenth shower, I think, did the trick—so that means we're ready for the second plan. Plus, this may well be the Greatest Idea a Young Male Has Ever Conceived and Executed since great ideas started to be kept track of."

Riley was only half listening as he mentally tabulated the essentials he had in his backpack—his first-aid kit, seven dollars and eighty-nine cents in loose change, a ball of twine, a Swiss Army knife, a roll of duct tape, a small radio, his old walkie-talkies, extra batteries and his last will and testament. He hadn't known of Henry's camping trip, of course; this was standard gear he never left the house without because he believed in always being prepared. For any eventuality.

"Here's the plan," Henry said. "We head into the bush down on the river, and for two days we make shelter, we find food, we live as one with the great outdoors, just like our pioneer, um, what's that word? Forefathers. Is this a great idea or what?"

"Wait, wait." Reed tried once more. "How about if the idea of wilderness is more like camping in the backyard? And it's okay to go inside and watch TV, eat Twinkies, use the bathroom? Maybe even sleep in the house when it gets dark and cold or the bugs come out? That seems more 'us' than the woods and no-supplies thing."

"What sounds like you, sissy boys, is going shopping at the mall with my little sister for training bras and lip gloss." Dwight Hauser had been lurking around the corner, eavesdropping. He had three of his mindless goons with him.

"Hello, Dwight," Henry said. "Listening in on other people's conversations again? Don't you have anything better to do?"

"You mean like you guys? Playing camp in the woods? You'll last twelve minutes before Reed here pees himself and Riley walks into a tree because he's got his head stuck in a book. Dweebs and brainiacs and whatever it is *you* are, Mosley, can't handle the outdoors."

"Thanks for your feedback, Hauser—we needed

the input of a moron. Run along now and take your sycophants with you. That means 'brainless followers,' by the way," Riley said, leading Reed and Henry down the hall and out the door.

"Nice one, Riley. You have the greatest vocabulary," Henry said.

"Did you see how confused they looked when Riley called them sicko-whatsits?" Reed was practically bouncing with excitement. "I've been waiting for a moment like that since first grade when Dwight told me the paste pot was full of cake frosting. I'll show him I can camp outside. What do you think, Riley?"

"I want to see what happens. I'm in."

"It's unanimous!" Henry beamed. "We'll head to the woods immediately after school. The great thing is—no preparation necessary. This is probably the easiest plan I've ever come up with. Oh, wait! Reed, call home and tell your folks you're sleeping at Riley's. Riley, tell your folks you're staying at my place. And I'll tell my parents I'm at Reed's."

Reed and Riley both nodded; Reed's house was so full of girls he wouldn't be missed, and although Riley was an only child, his parents were always happy when he was out with his friends instead of sitting in his room with a book. Henry's parents breathed a little easier and slept a little deeper when they didn't have to worry about what plans he was concocting under their roof—ever since the vinegar and baking soda incident in the garage that had forced Henry's parents to call the police hazmat teams and park their cars in the driveway for a whole summer.

Henry smiled through the rest of his classes, daydreaming about campfires, and lean-tos made of sticks and leaves and dried mud. Reed went to the restroom twelve times and wondered: Could you possibly get frostbite in May? Riley spent the afternoon free period in the library researching native nuts and berries that were safe to eat and brushing up on his recognition of poison oak and poison ivy.

They met up under the flagpole after the final bell rang and started walking toward the edge of town. No one talked very much. Gradually the residential neighborhoods turned into run-down industrial complexes, and then they found the rail yard. After checking his map, Henry pointed them toward a rail line that ran away into the woods.

"Why is it so dark? Is it always so dark in the

wilderness?" Reed said as the sun started to dip below the horizon. He stumbled on a rock, a root or a poisonous snake. He wasn't sure which. Just in case, he jumped about six feet straight up. "I've never seen so much darkness, even when I close my eyes at night. But that's probably because Amy, my second-littlest sister, is so afraid of the dark that we leave the bathroom light on. And the light in the hall. And the one on the stairway. So it's never, you know, ever really dark at my house."

"You talk a lot when you're nervous," Riley said.

"It took a lot longer to get here than I thought," Henry finally admitted. "But anyone can set up a camp in the daylight with gear; it's really something to be out here with nothing in the dark. We need to find a campsite quick, though, before things start to go wrong. Not that I think they will, of course. I have a gut feeling that everything is going to work out for us this weekend."

There was an enormous splash followed by a sputtering scream, then a gurgle and the sound of a bunch of brush breaking and, finally, a thump as if something large and wet had dropped from a great height into thick mud.

"I found the river," Reed called.

"Good," Henry said. "Now we know we aren't going to die of thirst."

"I'm not sure that's the most sanitary suggestion," Riley pointed out. "Do you know what Connor Howes did in this river after he drank eighteen sodas during the Scout camp-out last year?"

"Too late," Reed said from the darkness. "I've already swallowed about a gallon. So I don't want to hear any more about Connor and the river of pee."

"Oh, come on, men," Henry said. "This isn't so rough. It's not like there are bears and moose and mosquitoes and other things that want to eat us. We're out here in the tame woods where nothing can go wro—"

He was interrupted by a deep, coughing, gacking, growly sound that seemed to shake the leaves on the trees.

Even Henry was silent. Then Reed, who had squelched back to his friends by following the sound of Henry's voice, leaned in and whispered, "What was that?"

"Probably some kind of night bird. Yeah. I saw a video where night birds sounded just exactly like that. So I'll bet that was it, then. A night bird. Just

32

a bird. A small, vegetarian bird who won't swoop too close to us or rake us with her talons or carry us back to the nest in her beak to feed, alive and squirming, to her babies."

There was a second coughing growl, much closer, and within an instant, an insane laugh.

"I smell doody again," Reed said. "Brand-new, though, and right behind me. Like it's following me."

They heard another frightening laugh, followed by a bone-rattling howl. A high-pitched shriek made them jump and then a cataclysmic whoosh roared through the darkness as something huge splashed in the river.

At this precise instant, Riley decided to pull out the small penlight he had taped to his leg for emergencies. It wasn't that he was afraid, although he worried that certain of his bodily functions were coming close to being uncontrollable; rather, he just wanted to know why night birds would seem so (a) loud, (b) big and (c) plentiful. In some measure he would, for the rest of his life and especially during REM sleep after he'd had too much sugar or caffeine, regret this decision.

He turned the light on and the three boys found themselves looking at a full-size Bengal tiger. Standing 3.6 feet away.

Riley flicked the light off.

He counted to three, took a deep breath, prayed for a night bird and turned the light back on.

The tiger stood motionless for a moment before opening his mouth and baring teeth that looked a yard long.

Before Reed could even whimper, something waist high and covered with stinking hair poked him in the back, whuffled a loud chuckling sound, grabbed him by the seat of the pants and headed off through the undergrowth, dragging him along by his back pocket.

"Call 9-1-1!"

Riley and Henry couldn't even turn to watch Reed disappear into the brush. They stood frozen, staring at the tiger. He stared back at them.

Meanwhile, Reed kicked and twisted free of his pants and the monster that had him by his back pocket. He fell in the dirt, rolled twice and crouched in the darkness, frantically looking around for whatever had grabbed him and then had, just as suddenly, disappeared.

"I'm free," he assured Riley and Henry, certain they were frantic with fear for him. "Don't worry. I got away."

He stood, pantsless, trying to catch his breath and figure out which way to trot back to Henry and Riley. Before he could move, though, something slithered out of the darkness and wrapped around his bare leg, holding tight. He looked down and saw what he thought was a gray anaconda, about half a foot thick.

"Hey," he called to Henry and Riley, suddenly and insanely calm, "a second monster thing just grabbed me. It's got me by the leg. I'm not free anymore."

Then the gray snakelike thing yanked him into the brush near the riverbank and the calm deserted him and he screamed, *"Henreeeeeeeeeeeeeeeeeeeeeeee!"*

Riley cast the flashlight beam toward the river, where he and Henry saw a half-naked Reed being swung through the air and then plunged back under the surface of the water, then up again, then under again, then up. Between dunks in the muddy pee-water, he screamed: *"Call* [dunk] *nine* [dunk] *one* [dunk] *one!"*

In the weak glow of the penlight, Henry and

Riley could see only a gray wall and one bright eye behind Reed.

The tiger, which had swung his head to watch Reed, turned back to the two boys, cough-growled again and moved forward, putting his front paws on Henry's shoulders and licking the top of his head with a rough, wet tongue. Then the tiger nuzzled the side of Henry's face, looking for all the world like an enormous house cat.

"Man, he seems to like you," Riley said. "Or maybe he's just tasting you. No, he's definitely being friendly; that doesn't look like a hungry kind of licking. Freaky, though, huh? To run into a tiger in the woods of surburban Cleveland? Not as weird as the thing that's got Reed, though."

About then Reed broke away from what he was thinking must be the sinister Boy-Eating, Water-Dwelling Snake Creature of Cleveland. Reed clambered up the riverbank and hit the ground running full-speed, at what Riley's report later estimated was 37.2 miles per hour. He crashed into hanging limbs, tree trunks, anthills, rocks and bushes, leaving thick clouds of doody odor in his wake and emitting bloodcurdling screams that echoed in the darkness.

As Henry and Riley and, of course, the tiger stood listening to Reed's terrified bellows, which were becoming more and more distant, a stocky man in khaki pants and a T-shirt that proclaimed EAT PLANTS, NOT ANIMALS suddenly emerged from the darkness. He was carrying a huge flashlight and leading a hyena on a leash.

"I'm Amazing Dave, owner of Amazing Dave's Wild Animal Show. We're traveling around the Midwest. A couple of cages got unlocked by mistake and some of our troupe wandered away. This is Mizzen, my hyena, and I think she ate your buddy's pants before I caught her. You've already met Nick here—and I thank you for not scaring him, he's kind of timid. Before he started running around yelling like that, your friend was playing in the water with Simon the elephant. Simon has a game with his handler where he dunks him underwater; he thinks everybody likes to play."

Dave stuck his fingers in his mouth and let loose with a piercing whistle. They heard a thumping splash and some crashing of bushes and Simon lumbered out of the darkness. He draped his trunk around Riley's shoulders and turned to watch Nick kiss Henry's scalp.

"They seem to like people." Riley petted the elephant's shoulder. "I mean they didn't, you know, like, eat us. Like one might normally expect from wild animals."

Dave smiled. "They're very affectionate and used to being around people. Mizzen here particularly likes chocolate—did that other boy have candy bars in his pockets? That may be why she grabbed his pants. And then ate them. Sorry about that."

"We weren't supposed to bring anything with us for the weekend camping trip I planned, but Reed does like chocolate. . . ." Henry trailed off, realizing how self-righteous he sounded. "We were practicing wilderness survival."

"Since our animals sort of messed up your camping trip, on behalf of Amazing Dave's Wild Animal Show, I'd like to invite you to stay with us this evening."

Reed's screams were growing fainter and fainter. Henry cupped an ear with his palm, listening intently, then shook his head. "We'd like to, we really would. But we'd better go after Reed. He sounds like he's halfway to Canada."

"Some other time, then," Dave said. "You can meet the other animals. I have a howler monkey named Pixie that your running friend would probably enjoy—they sound exactly alike."

Henry and Riley didn't catch Reed in the woods. By following the sound of his screams, they finally found him on the outskirts of town, hiding in some bushes next to a farm implement dealer.

"I don't want to complain or whine or anything," Reed said from underneath a lilac bush, "but man, that was some pretty wild stuff back there. First off, that furry laughing bear thing tried to eat my butt, and then that gigantic snake thing tried to drown me. It was kind of like that time in kindergarten when Dwight Hauser and I were taking swimming lessons together and he used me as a flotation device, only I didn't. Float, that is."

"You were amazingly brave," Riley assured Reed, and dragged him out from under the lilac bush.

"You think?" Reed looked thoughtful. "Is that what brave feels like?"

"Yup," Henry said. "It's kind of like sheer terror, only with a whole lot of adrenaline. And a happy ending."

Henry gave Reed his jacket to tie around his waist and cover what was left of his underwear. They started walking home in the darkness.

"This report," Riley said, "ought to be a corker."

"It could have been worse," Reed said as he trudged along behind Henry and Riley, his voice scratchy and raw from approximately three and a half miles of screaming. "I didn't wind up completely covered in doody this time. I lost my pants, but I saved my underwear. Or most of it. And I escaped from a scary thing that ate my pants, and got away from another scary thing that wanted me dead. Or at least really clean. How did you guys get away from that tiger, anyway?"

"Luck," Henry said. "Just luck. All the planning in the world, men, can't compare to perfectly timed good luck."

4

Night of the
Living Sludge

"Men," Henry announced to Reed and Riley during lunch the next week, spritzing air freshener in Reed's direction because he still smelled a little funky, "we are going to spend the night in a Dumpster."

Reed grabbed the air freshener and shot it back at Henry. "I still say I'm not the only one who smells bad; you must have stepped in tiger poo or else the tiger spit reacted with your shampoo. Did you just say you want us to sleep in a garbage can?"

Riley pushed aside his soup and pulled out his notebook to start outlining Henry's new plan.

"This was not originally on my list of possible activities to pursue," Henry confessed, gesturing to his yellow legal pad. "But I was sitting in Investigative Science this morning listening to Ms. Trudy's lecture about the environment when I realized that scientific experimentation is the Highest Form of Discovery and Personal Growth. To learn, to find, to know—to use science to uncover mysteries. What could be more exciting and interesting than that?"

"And you think spending the night surrounded by garbage is scientific?" Riley asked.

"Sure. Haven't you ever wondered about the contents of Dumpsters and trash cans and garbage buckets and wastepaper baskets?"

"No," Reed said. "I have never once thought about what gets thrown away."

"Neither had I. And I can't believe we've overlooked something so essential and meaningful. Besides, up to now our activities have been Lacking in Practical Application, not to mention Cultural Significance. This task will lead us toward not only getting science scholarships for college but also saving the world, one garbage heap at a time."

Reed looked doubtful and went back to his

sandwich. But Riley pulled out the catalog for a local university that he carried in his backpack because he believed in being prepared for every eventuality. He flipped to the section on scholarships.

"Henry's right. There's a scholarship contest for"—Riley began to read—"'the study of environmental protection by middle school students. The requirements: undertaking an original experiment, which must be totally self-directed, depending completely on the support and guidance of one's peers, and the submission of a paper detailing the hypothesis, experiment, results and conclusions, as well as suggestions for bettering society.'" He looked up. "We could totally do this. I want to see what happens. I'm in."

Henry said, "Yes! This is about your future, men. I knew this idea was perfect for us. I'm glad we're all in agreement." He wrinkled his nose and spritzed air freshener in Reed's direction again. "Now, about the division of labor—"

"Let me guess." Reed folded his arms. "You're doing all the idea-making and hypothesizing and Riley here is writing up the scholarship application afterward, which leaves me to be the one to actually sleep with the garbage."

"Oh, you won't be sleeping," Henry said, "you'll be too busy collecting specimens. And it won't be all night. You just need to scoop up a few samples of different kinds of waste for us to catalog and identify and experiment upon. That part we'll all do together."

"I don't know why we can't do the whole collection thing together, too. I already smell baby doody every minute of every day. I think the contents of that diaper got slammed up into my brain and the river pee burned into me on a cellular level because, when I sweat in gym class, I smell it really bad."

"See?" Henry nodded. "You're the ideal candidate for this part of the project. And, if it makes you feel any better, I'm going to be gathering specimens from the recycling bins at the same time."

Reed looked satisfied and Riley carefully penciled into his notes, "Reed: rancid garbage. Henry: old newspapers."

Henry continued: "There's a huge Dumpster outside school that we can use for our research—just think of all the good stuff from the home ec kitchens. We're in luck, too, because the eighth-grade science section is covering dissection this week, starting with frogs and working up to fetal pigs, so the science labs will throw away lots of interesting garbage. Furthermore, I happen to know from eavesdropping on the cafeteria ladies while I was in the lunch line that the new and improved super-nutritional menu is not meeting with approval from the student body and the disposal rate is unacceptably high."

"Um, excuse me." A soft voice broke into their conversation. They looked up and saw Marci Robbins standing next to their table, blushing furiously. "I wasn't trying to listen in on your conversation, but I happen to know that Ms. Meyers, the art teacher, is working on creating a new kind of biodegradable modeling clay with her classes and it's not going well. Or maybe too well. Statues are rotting while the students make them."

The only thing more astonishing than being helped out in their plan was being talked to by Marci Robbins, who was so painfully shy that she hardly ever spoke in class.

"Hey, thanks, Marci, that's good stuff," Henry said.

"A perfect wet-to-dry ratio," Riley said, nodding.

"Do you want to come with us?" Reed asked hopefully.

"Oh, no." Marci looked horrified. Or terrified. The boys couldn't tell. "I just, well, wanted to be helpful. Good luck with your project and, um, the whole odor thing you've got going here. I think your idea sounds fascinating." She practically ran out of the lunchroom.

"That's the most words I've ever heard from Marci in all the years we've been going to school together," Reed said, looking after her as she fled.

Riley nodded. "She's good people."

"Let's meet this evening after dinner and get to work," Henry said.

"Today is always your favorite day of the week to start a plan." Reed sighed.

"You might stop stinking if we don't get going this evening, and that would be a waste of perfectly good stench," Henry said before he and Riley put their heads together to reread the experiment standards and protocols in the catalog.

"Well, sure, when you put it that way." Reed carried his lunch bag over to the trash, dropped it in, peered down and said into the bin, "See you later."

*   *   *

Henry and Riley were pacing next to the Dumpster outside the cafeteria that evening, waiting for Reed to show up. They had told their parents they were meeting at the library to work on a science project, which was mostly true and more likely to be agreed to than asking for permission to go Dumpster diving.

Finally, they heard a rustling noise from the darkness and turned to see Reed hurrying toward them. He was wearing a rain poncho and waterproof trousers reaching from his armpits to attached rubber boots.

"Good thinking, Reed," Henry said. "I should have mentioned protective gear. I like the way you wrapped your entire body in plastic cling film before you put your clothes on—that was smart, because you can't, after all, be too safe. You didn't, by any chance, ask your mother when your last tetanus shot was, did you? Not"—he hurried on—"that you'll need it, but it's always good to know."

Henry slapped a headlamp from his dad's last camping trip onto Reed's forehead as Riley slid a backpack over Reed's shoulders. He'd filled it with small glass vials and Ziploc bags from his home science kit. Then Henry handed Reed a plastic bucket with a lid for scooping up the mushy bottom layer from the Dumpster, and Riley gave him a stick to stir the more interesting garbage around.

"Now, remember," Henry instructed Reed, "we need a wide sample—solids, liquids, whatever that oozy, sludgy stuff is leaking out the bottom. Don't come out until you've filled the tubes and jars and Ziploc bags and that bucket with research material. I'm heading over to the recycling bin to gather a selection, and Riley's going to crawl in through the window of the science lab that I propped open with a textbook earlier today and get started on the report. You and I will meet up back here in one hour, at precisely twenty-one hundred hours, with our specimens and head to the lab to start the experiments together."

Reed sighed, pulled his uncle's scuba mask over his eyes and nose, adjusted the painting mask he'd found in the garage over his mouth, yanked on the yellow rubber gloves his mother used to do the dishes, and climbed into the Dumpster. He was about to ask Riley to check him for exposed sections of skin when Henry flipped the lid shut and

Reed was plunged into total darkness. He heard Riley's and Henry's footsteps getting fainter.

He hadn't been in the Dumpster three seconds when he knew he wasn't alone.

He reached up and flipped the switch on the headlamp. Eyes shone at him from the other end of the Dumpster. The eyes were yellow.

He moved his head so the light no longer hit what he decided was either a very large rat or a very small rhino. In either case, the garbage-eating beast stayed at the other end, and Reed decided to focus on collecting trash as quickly as he could while hoping the rhino-rat didn't have family and friends in the Dumpster. The thing looked, Reed thought, a little like Dwight Hauser, with the same kind of hulking presence and small, mean eyes. Except he'd bet the rhino-rat had a better personality. Bacterial fungus, he thought, had a better personality and made more interesting company than Dwight Hauser.

The first thing he saw when he looked down was food from the cafeteria. My mother, he thought, would have an absolute fit if she knew how many vegetables got thrown away from the lunch trays.

"If you don't eat your vegetables," she said at every meal, "and chew them properly, you'll lose your teeth. Then your thinking will become muddled, causing you to forget how to spell and do basic math, after which you'll flunk out of school. Without a proper education, you will never get a decent job, and sooner or later you can count on winding up in prison or living in a Dumpster."

He heard a new sound, whispered "Call 9-1-1" to make himself feel better and tried to convince himself it was merely the rhino-rat, busily eating disposed-of vegetables in order to get big and strong as it sat quietly off to the side, watching Reed collect garbage.

He carefully bagged seven blackened carrots, three moldy snow peas, a clump of corn Niblets that hung together mysteriously and two chicken nuggets that squirmed with something small, white and alive. He tossed a sandwich crust at the rhino-rat and then pawed through the first level of garbage to the next. He plucked several frog carcasses off the top of the layer and hoped they were from the biology lab and not the lunchroom. He grabbed a clump of something that looked like what the plumber had pulled from his sisters' shower drain last fall; he carefully sealed it in one of the larger Ziploc bags. He poked a plastic garbage bag with his stick and it burst open, a river of green and runny guinea pig, mouse, white rat, frog and turtle poop from the science labs spreading out across his feet. Oh, good, he thought: doody. Even the rhino-rat looked disgusted and edged farther away from Reed.

"Don't throw up. Don't throw up. Don't throw up. You'll just have to bag it for Henry," he chattered to himself. "Can't smell a thing, not scared at all, the rhino-rat isn't going to brush up against me because he's staying on his side of the Dumpster and I'm way over here, nothing just scurried across my foot, almost done, hate Henry, hate Riley, moving to Fiji . . ." He found that keeping up a running monologue prevented him from thinking too hard about the squishy goo and gelatinous muck he was getting to as he dug deeper.

He couldn't smell anything from behind his scuba and painting masks. The gloves and plastic wrap protected his skin from any direct contact, and he was beginning to feel almost comfortable flipping through the layers of crud and ooze, when he tossed aside a broken cafeteria tray and found a shimmering puddle of slimy, sludgy, not-quite-solid, not-quite-liquid, spongy semiorganic material that seemed to move away from him when he tried to scoop it up. Even the rhino-rat looked surprised at that. Reed searched for additional signs of life in the ooze and then decided that whatever it was, wasn't actually alive. He closed his eyes, reached down and slid his bucket through the middle of the puddle—it had the consistency of Jell-O and snot. He secured the lid on top. Done.

He climbed out of the Dumpster, dragging his bucket and backpack behind him. He waved good-bye to the rhino-rat, slammed the cover on the Dumpster and sat down to wait for Henry. He pretended not to hear the sudden increase in noise inside the Dumpster. He imagined that microscopic crawly things were slithering all over his skin under the plastic wrap. Maybe I've got the plague, he thought, or parasites or lice or rhino-rat cooties.

Henry finally showed up with neat paper bags full of tidily folded newspapers and empty soda cans. Henry padded silently, while Reed squished and sloshed with every step, through the darkened school hallways to the science labs.

Riley had flipped on a computer and pulled up the rough draft of the paper he'd started working on that afternoon in study hall. He was surrounded by open textbooks and pages of handwritten notes and had a second and a third computer logged on to different search sites. He zoomed between the computers on a wheeled desk chair.

Henry set his bags on a lab table and started to sort through them. He pulled out newspapers and magazines and clucked disapprovingly when he found a plastic pudding cup from the faculty lounge.

Reed dragged his bags of specimens to a table in the corner and started undressing. He threw the poncho and waders and scuba mask and painting mask and rubber gloves and miles of plastic wrap that he unwound from his body into the hazardous-materials disposal bin at the back of the room.

Once Reed was stripped down to his bottom layer of regular clothes, which he noted were miraculously clean and dry and stench-free, and had assured himself that nothing tiny, alive and dangerous was crawling around on him, he stepped over to the table where his specimens were and, with a sense of confidence he didn't usually feel, started to pry the lid off the bucket.

"We need—" Henry was going to say more, but he couldn't. Because, as Riley later wrote in his follow-up report, someone had left a Bunsen burner ever so slightly on after last-period science class, and the accumulated methane in the sealed bucket of shimmering, slimy, sludgy, not-quite-solid, not-quite-liquid, spongy semiorganic material that Reed had collected, ignited.

The contents of the bucket exploded upward, and the force of the blast carried Reed across the science lab, out into the hall and into a locker.

Except for a wave of glistening slime that stretched from the science table to the hallway, the lab wasn't damaged.

"I'm okay." Reed's voice echoed from the depths of the locker. "I'm wedged pretty tight, but nothing hurts and I'm not bleeding. Good thing we did this after school when no one was around, because we could have gotten in some serious trouble."

The contents of the bucket, now completely liquefied from the chemical reaction, dripped down the sides of the locker, drenching Reed but, as Henry later pointed out, making him slippery enough to pop right out of the tight space without even dislocating his shoulders or hips.

Other than some small paper cuts on his fingers, Henry was fine. Riley wasn't hurt except for a slight strain in his right ankle from zooming his desk chair into the hall to check on Reed.

"I reek of decomposition and fetid rot," Reed said sadly. "Remember the good old days when I just smelled baby doody with every breath and had the constant taste of river pee in my mouth?"

"Yeah, those were good times," Riley said absently as he jammed a flash drive into a computer and started adding to the report details about the minor explosion, eye-watering stench, shimmering wave of gunk and subsequent removal of Reed from the locker.

"I think, men," Henry said, "that this may be our finest hour. Reed, I'm sure I speak for Riley when I say: Another exceptional job on your part. Thanks for taking the lead on the heavy-lifting part of the experiment. You were great." Reed smiled and ducked his head modestly. "I read the directions carefully," Henry went on, "and there was nothing about the experiment being a success; we were only supposed to think of one, execute it and write it up.

We're three for three. Even if it's going to take us all night and every paper towel in the building to clean up the mess."

"Henry?" Reed said. "I don't want to worry anyone or sound like I'm whacked out or anything—but didn't it seem to you that the sludge we collected was alive somehow? I mean, it slithered when I tried to catch it and then it threw me across the building. Maybe whatever that was didn't want to be the subject of our experiment."

"We just won't mention that in our scholarship application," Henry decided. "No sense compromising the fine scientific research we've accomplished with superstitious fear that the discovery of a new life-form could raise. Besides, the blast probably killed it. All in all, a huge leap forward for the scientific method. I'm pretty sure this is how Galileo must have felt."

"Or Dr. Frankenstein," Reed said, still sure the sludge had moved away from him.

5

The Headless, Blood-Drinking, Flesh-Eating Corpses of Cleveland

"This time," Henry said, "I've come up with something really unusual." He was eating pizza with Reed and Riley in his backyard on a Saturday afternoon.

"Wait!" Reed said. "Do you think it's time for us to do another project when I still stink from the last three? I have to sleep in the basement and shower in the washtub in the laundry room because my mother says my smell is getting in her curtains and carpeting. I'm not supposed to do anything else interesting until the odor from the last three interesting things we've done stops seeping into her walls. I don't even know what this means, but she says I'm bringing down the value of the house and diminishing the equity my parents have built over the years because of how awful I smell."

"Uh-huh." Henry was nodding but not really listening.

"And I have to sit by an open window in every class and I can't eat lunch in the cafeteria anymore because the funk that surrounds me makes people sick to their stomachs. The only good thing is that Dwight keeps his distance, which, when you stop to think about it, is almost worth smelling baby doody all the time and constantly tasting river pee and always stinking like sludge."

"Mystery," Henry announced, ignoring Reed. "I am talking about mystery. We do not have enough mystery in our lives, men. We don't have *any* mystery in our lives. Let's change that."

"I think maybe Reed has a point, Henry," Riley said. "Your ideas have a weird way of making him smell really bad. And it's getting harder and harder to always keep downwind of him. Which reminds me: Reed, could you move 3.7 inches to your left? Because the wind has shifted slightly and I'm catching a whiff."

"This is different." Henry paused as he watched Reed shift over on the picnic table bench. "It's not a dangerous or smelly project. This time we're going to solve a mystery. We'll just be using our brains."

"I'm up for anything pain-free. And stench-free. Solving a mystery doesn't sound like it could hurt or smell," Reed said hopefully.

"We're going to solve a murder mystery that's over a hundred years old. When I was in the public library doing a social studies report, I found an old journal by a guy who lived in Cleveland in the nineteenth century. Turns out that the Hansen family, who lived out on the east edge of town, disappeared on May 8, 1887."

"What do you mean, 'disappeared'?" Riley asked, jotting "5/8/1887—family gone" in a small notebook he pulled from his pocket.

"On May seventh the whole family was seen sitting on the porch, waving at a neighbor on his way to town. But on May eighth, they were gone— the man, his wife, their fourteen-year-old daughter and even the dog. The house was completely empty."

"No one knows what happened?"

"Nope. The local lawmen investigated—

searched the house and grounds, asked the neighbors, talked to townsfolk, but no trace of them was ever found. No one ever heard from them again."

"And we're going to find them?" Reed asked.

"Yup."

"Now, over a hundred years later?"

"Yup."

"How's that going to work?"

"I have inside information they didn't have back then," Henry said.

"And what's that?"

"A note saying where the bodies were hidden."

"Bodies?" Reed drummed his fingers nervously on the tabletop. "Notes about bodies are never good. Hardly anything good ever comes from talking about bodies. We're getting back to the dangerous thing again, Henry. Next you'll be talking about worms. Worms that eat bodies and smell like decomposition and rot."

Henry pulled an old leather-bound volume from his backpack and held it up.

"'Darryl Dawson,'" Riley read from the cover. "'A Life Book.'"

"Dawson was a Clevelander whose descendants

donated his journals to the library because he had so diligently recorded what he heard and saw each day," Henry said. "But it wasn't the journal that was interesting as much as the note I found inside." Henry thumbed through the pages of his yellow legal pad until he located a loose piece of paper. "Here, read this."

Reed took it. "It's torn and the letters are smudgy and most of the page is missing." Riley leaned in to see.

"Read what's there."

". . . Bodies too difficult to bury . . . deposited in an old powder cavern . . ." Riley stopped. "How do you know this has anything to do with the missing family?"

"Read the date at the top of the page. What does it say?"

"May 7, 1887."

"And look at this, the clincher," Henry said. "Where they say they hid the bodies. An old powder cavern, right?"

Reed shifted nervously. "I don't even know what that means."

"I read an article about it. During the Civil War,

the Northern army had a storage depot here in Cleveland—a small cave at the riverbank that was excavated in order to store gunpowder. The headquarters for the supply depot where the army officers and clerks worked was the building that later became the Hansen house."

"So?"

"The cavern was expanded to run right under the headquarters building so that the army had access to the gunpowder supplies from the head-quarters. After the war, the cavern was shut down and abandoned and the tunnel that connected the building to the cavern was sealed off, and pretty much everybody forgot about it. Everybody, that is, except the killers of the Hansen family, because that's where they put the bodies."

Reed stared at him. "You're crazy, you know that, Henry? Stark nuts."

"But you're coming with me tonight, right?"

"Where?"

"To the old Hansen house—that old stone building past the highway."

"That place is supposed to be haunted!"

"We're not going to disturb any ghosts," Henry

said. "We're just going to be looking for the bodies of a murdered family."

"Oh, is that all?" Reed said.

"Absolutely. We owe it to the victims, men, to solve at least part of the mystery of their murders. We have to"—Henry dropped his voice reverently—"Give Peace to the Dead and Allow Them to Rest. It's Our Duty."

"How are we going to find the tunnel?" Riley asked.

"I dug around at the library and copied an old army drawing of the hidden entrance to the tunnel in the house. It's behind a wall in the basement, then you go down a ladder." Henry pulled a scribbled map out of his pocket.

"I don't know, Henry, this sounds kind of crazy. What do you think, Riley?"

"I want to see what happens. I'm in."

"Perfect," Henry said. "I knew you guys would love this idea."

"I'm not going anywhere alone, I'm not doing anything dangerous and I am not going near anything that stinks," Reed said.

"Of course not," Henry said. "We'll be as safe as

if we stayed home. We're all sticking together and doing the exact same thing at the exact same time. What could possibly go wrong?"

"When you put it that way, it does sound like a good plan," Reed said. "Very cool."

Riley wrote down "safe" and then a question mark in his notebook, but he didn't say anything.

A few hours later they were outside the Hansen house, which stood on an untended, brushy lot. They were running out of excuses to give their parents for breaking curfew, so each of them had climbed out his bedroom window.

The sky was black with storm clouds, and drops of rain were beginning to fall. The front door of the house was gone and half the front wall was caved in.

"Take these," Riley said, digging into his backpack. "I brought Night Commander flashlights." He also pulled out a book about paranormal activity, because brushing up on ghost protocol and etiquette seemed like a good idea prior to entering a bone-laden storage tunnel underneath a haunted house. Riley believed in being prepared for any eventuality.

"Now," Henry said, "according to the drawings I

studied, there's a stairway just inside the front door leading to the basement. At the bottom of the steps, we head to the right, to the sealed-in space behind a wall that leads farther down, to the old cavern underneath the house where the bodies are located."

"Tell me again," Reed said, "why we didn't just call the police and let them know about the bodies you think we're going to find?"

"Because then we wouldn't get any credit for breaking the case," Henry said. "And it's not solving the mystery if you just help the police. We have to do it ourselves. Or it doesn't count and it's not a real adventure. Now come on."

Since there was no front door, they climbed over the threshold and, a few tentative feet later, found themselves at the top of the stairway to the basement, which was missing more risers than it still had. The ones that still clung between the wall and the disintegrating railing looked wobbly. Henry put his foot on the partially rotted wood of the first step gingerly. "This way . . . easy now."

The instant all three boys were on the stairs, the old square-cut nails that held the stairway together gave out and what was left of the stairs collapsed.

As Riley later wrote in his report, gravity being what it was, the boys dropped like stones to the basement floor, where they expressed their sudden stop in terms of high G-loads that quadrupled their effective weight and brought the load to an instantaneous 0.7 tons—after which the rotting basement floor also gave way. They plunged into the cavern below as if they'd been shot through a cannon.

They came to rest in front of a pile of old bones that stood nearly eight feet tall and seven feet wide, gleaming white, horribly white, in the glare of their Night Commander flashlights.

"We found the bodies, men," Henry said.

"That's a whole lot of bones," Reed said.

"How big was the family, again?" Riley asked. "Because this seems like more than a husband and wife and daughter and dog. Even if it was a large dog. Even if it was a doggysaurus."

"Oh, man," Reed said, "this is just like that zombie movie about the headless, blood-drinking, flesh-eating corpses. There was a stairway in an old deserted house, just like this, that led down into a pit, just like this, where the zombies kept the bones of their victims after they had drained all the blood and eaten all the flesh. Just. Like. This."

For a few seconds, they stood silently, Riley trying to count the bones for inclusion in his report, Henry peering past the bone pile, hoping there were other discoveries to be made, and Reed trying to remember what had happened to the people from the zombie movie who found the bodies that the headless, blood-drinking, flesh-eating corpses had eaten, when they heard . . . *eee ah, eee ah, eee ah*, faintly from the depths of the tunnel that led out of the cavern.

"That's exactly the sound," Reed breathed, "that the headless, blood-drinking, flesh-eating corpses made as they zeroed in on their victims."

"Don't be sil—" Henry started to say, but he was cut off by the sudden flapping of hundreds of dark wings that filled the pit where they stood.

"Bats, it's bats, they're bats, bats are flying at my head!" Reed screamed. "Call 9-1-1! Bats carry rabies and I'm afraid of giant needles being stuck in my belly if I get rabies!" He dropped his Night Commander flashlight and started blindly running away from the bats, which had been disturbed by the boys' noise and flashlights. Henry and Reed ducked and doused their lights but remained still and relatively calm.

Reed's shrieks bounced off the walls of the tunnel, matching the impact of his body. Blind and terrified in the sudden pitch dark, Reed ran deeper and deeper into the tunnel and slipped on the suddenly gooey, slick floor, cartwheeling off the sides of the tunnel before landing in a soft, wet pile that smelled like ammonia and decaying flesh.

"I found the zombie poop," he called. "I can't see because the smell is making my eyes water, but I'm okay. I can't hear because my ears are packed full and I'm pretty sure it's leaching into my brain cavity, but I'm okay. And it's burning my scalp and it feels like my hair is falling out in clumps, but I'm okay. Can you guys, uh, come find me and help me out? Because I don't mean to worry anyone or complain, but even though I'm okay, I'm afraid to move right now."

"It's like he has a gift," Henry said to Riley as they flipped on their flashlights and made their way down the tunnel toward Reed's voice. "No matter where we go or what we do, he's like a compass pointing north when it comes to locating smelly goo."

"Extraordinary," Riley agreed. "You work so hard

to come up with these adventures and somehow it always comes down to Reed in a pile of poop."

The bones in the tunnel, Riley later discovered at the library, were buffalo bones that had been brought in by train during the last days of the great buffalo hunts, to be ground up for fertilizer. But the bone market had suddenly gone bust and, looking for a place to store them, the shippers had told their men to put the buffalo skeletons in the old cavern.

Riley also investigated and found the Hansens' names on a passenger list for a ship bound for South America, where they had gone to work on a cattle ranch. He put all this in his report.

And the zombie poop was really bat guano, which, Reed later discovered, while not blinding or deafening or hair-removing, did seem to have a tenacious odor that everyone had some trouble getting used to. Although he could no longer smell himself. Or anything else, for that matter.

His mother ordered him to bathe in several gallons of tomato juice and insisted on burning his clothes in the backyard. She scheduled an appointment with a therapist so Reed could work through his issues about solid waste, and she spoke on the phone for a very long time with the family doctor about what symptoms to watch for in case Reed had contracted rabies, and then she found a website where she could purchase the unbleached organic cotton briefs that were recommended, along with liberal doses of ointment, to soothe the weepy blisters on the insides of his thighs that proved he was allergic to bat guano.

6

Cowboys
and Fishermen

"I've come up with our next project, men. Or I should say, the next two projects." Henry was walking home from school with Riley and Reed the week after the haunted house fiasco.

Riley jumped in front of Reed and threw his arms out protectively. "We're having enough trouble with one adventure at a time."

"Thanks, Riley, but the sores on my legs have pretty much healed, and I gotta tell you, I wonder what he's got in mind," Reed said. "I think I'm getting kind of hooked on the rush we get from doing these things."

Riley looked at him skeptically but stepped from between him and Henry. "Okay, Henry, what's the plan?"

"We need something bold, like two adventures at a time, to overcome the biggest mistake I've made so far. Think about it for a second: What's our worst dilemma?"

"The stench," Reed said.

"That's bad, sure, but the worst thing is that we haven't let anyone know about our adventures. We've been setting up all these cool things, but we haven't gotten any kind of reputation. This is the kind of stuff that Brings People Fame and Fortune."

"I posted every report on my blog, Henry," Riley reminded them.

"Yeah, and that's great. Maybe Reed and I never said anything, but we're both impressed by your online reports," Henry said.

"Yeah, and you never make me seem like a clueless dork, either, Riley," Reed added. "I always sound kind of fearless when you write about what I've done. And it's nice how you don't make too much about the whole stink factor."

"You're welcome," Riley said. "But I see Henry's

point: Even though I post all our adventures, we're not really getting the word out."

"Who would we want to tell?" Reed asked.

"Girls," Henry said. "The kinds of things we're doing would really help us to be more popular with girls, if they only knew about how . . . brave and um . . . creative and"—he nodded to Riley—"well documented we've been lately."

Riley nodded back. "None of us seem to be able to make any kind of decent connection with a girl."

"I don't know about you two," Reed put in, "but the only problem I have talking to girls is that I can't get close enough to a girl to talk. If she can hear me, she can smell me—no matter how many times my mother makes me scrub with special detergent and spread baking soda paste all over my skin to absorb the vile reek."

"Success with girls, I've figured out, is about image," Henry said, ignoring Reed. "I've been thinking about how we can change our image. We need something that Makes Us Attractive to the Opposite Sex. We should do something tough. Rugged."

"In suburban Cleveland?" Reed snorted. "Good luck."

"No, listen! My uncle has a farm out on the edge of Mud River, a couple of hundred acres," Henry said. "He invited us to spend the weekend."

Reed shook his head. "Farms mean animals. Animals mean poop. Me and any more poop means that my mother is going to move me out of the basement and into the garage because no one, she says, should have to live with the kind of smells that I bring back from your adventures."

"There are supposed to be some giant catfish in the river," Henry went on, remembering not to breathe through his nose near Reed. "They live in the mud along the bottom and get to be one, maybe two hundred pounds. I thought we'd take the old rowboat and some poles and catch one. Catching huge fish is macho."

"Fishing sounds okay, because water doesn't smell. But you said you had two projects."

"Oh, yeah." Henry nodded. "The rodeo. Everyone knows that cowboys have to beat girls off with sticks. Really, it's a stroke of genius—I wonder why I didn't think of it sooner."

"Genius?" Reed shook his head. "It sounds like the most painful thing ever. My dad took me to a rodeo when I was little, and I remember lots of blood and lots of things breaking. Things like arms and legs and heads."

"Nah," Henry said, "that's just to impress the audience. Nothing like that will happen to us."

"Rodeos," Riley pointed out, "are all about riding huge, violent, untamed animals and falling off them. Though"—he stopped to think—"one thing Reed is really good at is falling. He's almost as good at falling as he is at collecting horrific smells."

Reed nodded. And then, as if to prove his point, tripped over a crack in the sidewalk.

"I've already worked it out," Reed went on. "My uncle saved some old horses that were going to be put down after they retired from the rodeo circuit. He brought them back to his farm to let them live their lives out in a pasture alongside the river. He said they're completely tame, so old they're nearly blind, and as gentle as kittens. We can ride them this weekend."

"Riding a couple of old horses doesn't sound so bad," Reed said. "Especially if you and Riley do the riding and I just watch. Clean and safe."

"Even if we don't do actual tricks," Henry said, "riding old rodeo horses will be bound to impress all the girls. Or some girls. Maybe just one girl . . ."

"And how do we make sure the girls find out?" Riley asked. "No one's reading the blog."

"We'll take a lot of pictures," Henry said. "No matter what happens, there are sure to be at least a few shots that look really good, full of action. We pick the best ones and start showing them around school."

"I want to see what happens. I'm in," Riley said.

"I'd like to go fishing, but I'm not going anywhere near the manure. Count me out," Reed said firmly. "Because you know what? I've been thinking, and I think girls will like me if I learn to stand up for myself and stop doing things that could seriously injure me and make me smell."

"Sure, Reed. We'd never make you do anything you didn't want to," Henry said. "So it's settled. My mom will drive us to my uncle's farm this weekend and we'll go fishing and ride broncs."

"He doesn't look so scary," Reed said. It was Saturday morning and the boys were leaning on the top rail of a fence behind the barn, looking at the bull. He was in a pen next to the one that held the two horses that Henry and Riley were going to ride.

"Are you sure he's even alive?" Riley asked. "He's just standing there, staring at the dirt."

"Well," Henry answered, "Uncle Joe said he's pretty old. But still alive—see, he's breathing. His name is Willard and he's super-mellow, like a milk cow, really. Little girls used to ride him at carnivals and county fairs. They'd put a ladder against his side and let the kids climb up and sit on him."

"He does look mellow." Reed studied the bull.

"Uncle Joe said he wouldn't buck unless the bucking strap was tied around his withers." Henry looked at Reed. "You sure you don't want to climb on and see what it's like? Just for a quick picture? You'll be on and off in ten seconds, tops. A photo of you sitting on a bull would be better than one of us just riding old rodeo horses."

"Yeah," Reed said. "I can do that. Ten seconds. What could happen in ten seconds?"

Henry gave Reed a boost onto the bull's back. "Settle into the shoulder just back of the hump. And wrap the end of the rope around your wrist—that's how the pro riders do it."

Riley pulled his camera out of his backpack. Henry mounted one of the two saddled horses in the next pen and eased him near the fence to get into the shot with Reed on the bull.

At first Reed was tense, but the huge bull stood quietly, breathing gently beneath Reed, his chest going in and out like a giant bellows. Peaceful, really, Reed thought.

"Gig him in the ribs with your heels," Henry called. "Just enough to get him to move out of the shadows so that Riley can take a really good shot in the sunlight. I'll be in the background on the horse."

Reed tentatively nudged the bull's ribs and felt Willard move—a mountain of flesh—one slow step forward. So far, so good, he thought, and smiled for Riley, who was shooting pictures as fast as his shutter would click.

Riley backed toward the fence surrounding the pen to get a better shot. It was an electric fence, and his hip brushed against the wire. The current made him jerk backward so hard that the wire broke and the end snapped forward and up, slapping Willard's rear with a good jolt of electricity approximately four and one half inches below where he pooped.

With what could only be called lightning speed,

Willard jumped straight into the air, so high, Riley wrote later in his report, that even though he looked like he probably weighed a full ton, he seemed to rise even with the roof of the barn. Willard cleared the fence around his pen and hit the ground running full speed toward the pasture where the cows grazed and, farther on, the river, which bordered the pasture.

Reed's wrist was still lashed to the bull's shoulder, but the rope began slipping as he ran. Now wrapped and tangled in the tail of the rope, Reed slid down Willard's side until he was flapping like a flag alongside the galloping bull.

Willard, being so old, probably would have stopped running, but Reed's screams of *"Call 9-1-1!"* so unnerved the bull, which was not used to rodeo cowboys bellowing for rescue, that he kept surging forward in a panic, trying to get away from Reed's piercing shrieks and flailing body.

The two old roping horses, bred and trained to chase running cattle, somehow found a few last ounces of their youthful strength, leapt the fence separating their pen from the pasture and tore off toward the river with insane speed in pursuit of Willard and Reed—one of them carrying

Henry, who was clutching the saddle horn with both hands.

As the horses sprinted to catch up with Willard, Reed—still tangled in the rope—slid until he was underneath the rampaging bull, being dragged through the mud and cow patties in the pasture.

All three animals flew off a three-foot bank and slammed into the murky mix of mud and slimy algae and dark water at the shallow edge of the Mud River. The rope that Reed was tangled in finally came loose, and he went flying another twenty feet before belly flopping in the middle of the river.

As Henry sat in the mud and watched, Reed clawed and spit and screamed and fought his way out of the water, clutching what later proved to be a seventy-four-and-a-half-pound catfish that, in a stroke of amazing luck, had happened to be lazily swimming directly underneath where he splashed into the river.

"I'm okay," Reed called. "I swallowed ten pounds of stuff I don't even want to think about—I mean, that *was* a pasture we went through—and underneath a bull is not the best place to ride, but I'm okay. I don't want to worry anyone or brag, but I think I caught an alligator when I landed in the water—I can't really see with all the mud in my eyes, plus I'm kind of afraid to look at what I'm holding. But I'm okay."

"I got the most awesome video and photos while you were being dragged on your face through the pasture," Riley hollered as he finally reached the riverbank. "This camera has an amazing zoom lens. I got you and the fish, too!"

"And you were worried about doing two plans at the same time." Henry wagged his finger at Reed. "You should have trusted that everything would work out. It always does. This may be our best adventure yet. Because being dragged upside down by a panic-stricken bull who was chased by two runaway horses and then landing on your face in the river and catching a ginormous catfish with your bare hands is the best possible outcome. I couldn't have planned it better. Is it just me, men, or do you think we have a real talent for adventure?"

"Adventure?" Riley said. "I'd say we're even better at disaster." He waded in to help Reed onto the riverbank.

Reed raised his fish in triumph. "We're the Masters of Disaster!"

7

The Last Great Race/Memorial Day Parade Disaster

THE DOGSLED PLAN
Final report and summary respectfully submitted
by Riley Dolen

The Dogsled Plan was launched at precisely 0900 hours, 43 minutes, on Saturday morning, 47 hours and 17 minutes prior to the Memorial Day parade, when Henry Mosley began to figure out the parade entry he and his friends Reed Hamner and Riley Dolen (author of this report) would submit this year.

Mosley's inspiration was a pack of seven dogs—a Rottweiler, a golden Lab, two Irish setters, a Border collie, a wire-haired terrier mix and a Chihuahua—the current client list of Hamner's fledgling dog-walking business. The dogs were tangled together and squirming and Hamner was patiently trying to untangle their leashes from each other when Mosley first conceived his parade entry idea.

Mosley suggested emulating the Iditarod, the dogsled race across Alaska, despite the facts that there hadn't been sufficient snow for a dogsled race in May in Ohio since the Ice Age and that access to the kind of sled dogs that traditionally run the race was sorely lacking. The willingness of Queso the Chihuahua, Kelly and Paddy the Irish setters, Glavine the Border collie, Wiley the terrier mix, Carl the Rottweiler, and Annie the golden Lab was taken as a given in the midst of Mosley's enthusiastic adoption of the dogsled concept.

Without securing the full support of his peers, Mosley devised a mock sled made of plywood, harnesses made of nylon webbing sewn together, and a gang line and tugs made of rope that would be hooked to the front of the sled. Having once read a book about dogsledding, Mosley insisted that clamping four skateboards underneath the mock sled would compensate for the lack of snow, but that complete control of the contraption would remain with the boys due to the addition of an old piece of carpet as a makeshift brake, fastened to the back of the sled with stout line.

Despite Hamner's reluctance to utilize the dogs from his business, Mosley prevailed by likening the parade to the daily walks on which Hamner was paid to take the dogs and suggesting that replacing the leashes with rope tugs tied to a gang line, and riding in the sled instead of walking with the dogs, would provide minimal disruption of the dogs' schedules and create absolutely no possibility for disaster.

Hamner and Dolen lacked the will to say no because (1) Hamner knew that one Erika Peterson and her synchronized skate team would be selling lemonade at the parade and (2) yours truly had a desire to see how everything turned out. The plan was reluctantly put into action.

The morning of Memorial Day was spectacular. The sun was shining, the sky was filled with puffy clouds and there was absolutely no evidence that later in the day a mixed herd of llamas, ponies and dogs would stampede through the front of the ice cream store, funnel out the back covered with rocky road ice cream and peach fat-free yogurt, swing around to the left and run amuck in the back alley before being rounded up by a mounted police force.

Initially, Mosley's plan unfolded smoothly, with the singular exception of the small tangle that forced Hamner to run alongside the dogs as they pulled the sled from his house down to the starting area because the house pets didn't know what a lead dog was. Well, Queso knew, but no other dog wanted to follow a Chihuahua. Especially when they were four times faster and fourteen times bigger than Queso.

At that point, Mosley was still insisting, "The whole thing is going to go like clockwork."

The parade stepped off from the community center at precisely 1000 hours, led by the veterans, the parade marshal and the mayor, all of whom were riding in convertibles.

Following the dignitaries were many papier-mâché–decorated floats representing various community organizations. The fire and police departments flashed lights and blasted sirens from their respective trucks and cars. The high school football team led the marching band and cheerleading squad from the school. A quilting club, a cooking class and a book group shared space on an antique steam engine. A group of five llamas and ten riderless ponies from the local petting zoo followed closely behind a small theatrical group from the after-school center's production of *Grease*. The dogsled, assorted tractors, collectible muscle cars and a motorcycle stunt team brought up the rear of what everyone later agreed could have been the best Memorial Day parade suburban Cleveland had ever seen.

At this juncture, it is important to mention that for years, the area at the center of the suburb had been the stomping ground of a domestic cat gone wild. Scarred from many battles, partially hairless from countless scrapes and gently confused as a result of his advanced age, Goren had used at least six of his nine lives and currently lived under a Dumpster near the ice cream store.

Despite being feral and half mad, Goren was surprisingly social and enjoyed a good parade as much as anyone else in town.

Mosley was at the rear of the sled, and Hamner was trotting along in front, confidently leading his dog team through the streets, waving to his relatives and friends and searching for signs of Erika Peterson and her synchronized skate team along the parade route as they approached the spot from which Goren had chosen to watch the parade—174 feet from the entrance of the ice cream store. When the dogs jogged past Goren, they were immediately behind the ponies, which were behind the llamas, which followed the assortment of theater students dressed up in poodle skirts and black leather jackets, singing an a cappella version of "We Go Together" with what this reporter can only call an excessive amount of "shang-shoo-bop"s.

The cat was quietly watching the parade; the dogs were enjoying being in the parade. Dwight Hauser, however, who has never enjoyed anything in his entire miserable, misbegotten life, had to go and ruin everything. This reporter, who was jogging alongside the dogsled, taking notes and snapping the occasional photo along with running the video camera, spotted Hauser, who spotted the dogs as they spotted the cat. Even so, nothing would have happened had Hauser's tiny mind not conceived an evil, vicious, malicious plan. Hauser leaned over as the dogs trotted by and said "Meow!" right into the ear of the Chihuahua.

The Chihuahua, obeying some genetic code that

makes even frail, tiny, practically decrepit dogs think and act as if they were a direct link to prehistoric pack-hunting wolves, leapt out of his ill-fitting harness. The standard-size harnesses afforded a great deal of wiggle room for Queso, and once freed, he tore after the cat.

The Chihuahua's explosive surge of speed and his bloodthirsty snarling and yipping triggered the Rottweiler's latent bloodlust. And Carl was a dog who couldn't resist a chase. His full-power lunge jerked the rest of the team ahead, yanking Hamner off his feet and dragging him after the sled by the rope tied to his waist.

As the sled jumped forward, the rug-brake was jerked from beneath Mosley's feet and he fell into the sled on his face, his feet kicking in the air.

Perched on top of four sets of free-rolling skateboard wheels, and unencumbered by Hamner acting as lead dog or Mosley exerting pressure on the rug-brake, the dogs streaked through the middle of the parade like a jet-powered train.

The team and the sled plowed directly into the pack of llamas, which got tangled up with the herd of ponies, which tripped the grade school singers, all of whom became entwined in the dogs' gang line.

The entire spitting, braying, barking, screaming, singing mass headed for Goren.

While he was normally willing to enter into battle with all real and perceived threats, Goren knew he was outnumbered, and adopting discretion as the better part of valor, he ducked down and headed for the nearest escape route.

Which, at that moment, proved to be the open door of the ice cream store, from which the Reverend Potter Jenks was emerging with his annual Memorial Day treat (French vanilla covered with sprinkles on a handmade waffle cone). So involved was Reverend Jenks with managing the dripping cone that he did not see the large cat followed by llamas and ponies and dogs and singers and a makeshift dogsled with one boy upside down and another being dragged alongside by a rope tied around his waist. The cone, halfway to his mouth, was slammed into his face, blinding him as the hooved, pawed, barking, screaming, spitting, singing tsunami roared over him and into the store.

Witnesses, including this reporter, saw Goren make two quick loops of the shop pursued by the mob before he blew a hole through the exact center of the screen door leading to the back alley. He was followed immediately by llamas, ponies, dogs, rowdy theater students still singing, the sled and Mosley and Hamner, who later denied that they had screamed the whole time even though Lacey, the girl who worked at the ice cream store, testifies she clearly heard Hamner bellow "Call 9-1-1!" as she stood paralyzed, a cup of mango strawberry gelato melting in her hand.

The torn screen frayed the rope that attached Hamner to the dog team, but his momentum was such that, once freed, he flew straight toward the Porta Potti that the town fathers had placed in the alley for the parade crowd.

In the back alley, Goren streaked up a power pole, where he clung to the top by his claws, shaking. The rest of the animals, joyous but exhausted, milled around the alley underneath the pole, making it easier for the police's mounted unit to round up the still-spitting llamas, ice-cream-covered ponies and howling dogs while simultaneously freeing the musical actors from the melee.

Local law enforcement, in this observer's opinion, did a magnificent job and delivered each animal and minor back to its proper supervisor, a little the worse for wear to be sure, but in a surprisingly upbeat mood.

In the end, two boys rested upended in the deserted alley.

"Is it over?" Hamner called from underneath the tipped-over Porta Potti. "I think I'm okay, even though my head seems to have been propelled through a wall of this outside bathroom thingie and I am looking at the business end of the toilet seat, which makes it hard to breathe. And I don't mean to worry anyone or complain, but I think I got road rash when I was pulled along the ground after the dog team. Because there's a kind of burning and stinging and itching with isolated patches of numbness along the right side of my body."

"It was," Mosley said dreamily, "awesome. The noise was overpowering and the syncopated rhythm of so many different animals—and small children—was amazing! I hope Riley got this on video so we can watch it later. And is it just me, or do you think the community-access cable channel would leap at the chance to air that footage?"

"It'd be nice to be on TV," Hamner agreed. "A replay would fill in the gaps of what I may have missed when I was upside down and skidding after the dog team on my face."

Mosley went on, "It's like I said the last time: We're really getting good at this adventure stuff. And now the world, or at least the world that subscribes to our local community-access cable channel, will see how enterprising and take-charge we are." He climbed out of the sled and pried the Porta Potti door off Hamner's head. "I'm glad we decided we needed to shake things up. Best decision we ever made."

The videotape of the parade is submitted herewith as visual proof that the contents of this report are true and accurate to the best of this reporter's abilities.

Sincerely yours,
Riley Dolen

8

Propaganda
and Turtle Dregs

"It's the last day of school, men," Henry announced as he and Reed limped to the cafeteria for lunch. It was the day after the Memorial Day parade. Riley followed—not limping. "We need to make it special. And there's a wrong I've seen that we need to right. I have an idea."

"I don't know that I'm up for another plan so soon after the last one, Henry," Reed said. "Although being dragged along the parade route and through the ice cream store and out into the alley on my side by a dog team and a herd of ponies and a flock of llamas and several dozen musically inclined students seemed to lessen the constant smell of baby doody and fetid Dumpster rot and bat guano and cow pies, I think it's just because layers of my skin were removed. I don't think it's a good idea to do another plan until the scabs on the entire right side of my body have dropped off. Or at least reached the crusty, healing stage instead of this oozy, red open sore thing I've got going on."

"Yeah, that's pretty gross," Henry admitted. He watched Riley toss Reed a fresh tube of salve and pull some gauze bandages and tape out of his first-aid kit. "But the idea I have is psychological warfare. We do everything from a computer terminal in the library."

"No risk? No danger? No poop? Nothing that would keep me from moving out of the garage back to the basement and maybe even someday all the way back to my bedroom if I stop stinking and itching and oozing and crying in my sleep and periodically flinching like I am these days?"

"Nothing like that," Henry said. "You've been going through a rough patch, buddy. Way to take one for the team. You're an inspiration and, have I mentioned, really tough. Thanks."

Reed shrugged modestly and dabbed at the

scrape on his right wrist with a cotton ball dipped in hydrogen peroxide from Riley's first-aid kit.

"What wrong needs righting?" Riley asked, pulling his small digital voice recorder from his pocket and clicking it on so that he could capture every word, because not only did he like to be prepared for every eventuality, but he also wanted documentation of the way this idea had started, for purposes of comparison and contrast when he wrote up his final report. He took out a notebook and a pencil because he didn't trust the recorder as much as his own notes.

Henry pulled out of his backpack a flyer that he had ripped off the wall. It read DON'T RUN IN THE HALLS.

"Does that mean the halls on the third floor?" Riley asked. "Or all the halls in school? Or all the halls in all government buildings? Or maybe it's an overall suggestion for every hall in the whole wide world?"

"It's not the sign that bothers me," Henry said. "The sign just reminds me of what a huge bully Dwight Hauser is."

"Because he's big and mean and makes everyone in school do what he wants and his father has a ton of money and his mother intimidates all the other mothers in the parent volunteer group and he makes infectious diseases seem preferable by comparison and we can't stand him?" Riley asked.

"And because of the way he fed me bunny turds and told me they were chocolate-covered raisins when we were in kindergarten?" Reed asked with a touch of bitterness.

"Yes! Especially the rabbit droppings. People like him always get away with everything because no one ever stands up to them. The thing with the sign was really annoying because I was standing there this morning reading it and Hauser went barreling through the crowd like he was an armored tank blasting through a war zone. No reason, just because he could and thought it was funny to bounce people off the walls. And no one said anything to him even though the hall was full of teachers."

Henry took a deep breath. "Then he was mean to Marci Robbins." Reed and Riley winced. "He knocked her down when she got in his way and then he called her stupid and laughed like it was a big joke when she started to cry."

"That scum." Riley put down his pencil.

Marci Robbins was sweet and quiet and so painfully shy that she blushed bright red when teachers called on her and stammered when she had to speak in front of the class and had probably never done anything wrong to anyone even once in her entire life. Plus, ever since she had contributed some helpful information while they were planning the Dumpster experiment, Riley had been keeping an eye on her; any girl with the powers of observation she had shown was interesting to him. And he'd noticed how pretty she was, too.

"I'm in," Riley said, closing his notebook.

"What do you have in mind?" Reed asked.

"This afternoon is field day; since we finished our tests and turned in our books this morning, we're supposed to do PE outside all day. But I say we ditch that and hole up in the library."

"And?"

"And come up with some flyers of our own."

Riley opened his backpack and pulled out a ream of retina-searing fluorescent-yellow copy paper. "Aren't you glad now that I'm always prepared for every eventuality?"

Henry grinned. "Flyers printed on paper that color will really attract attention."

*   *   *

Henry, Riley and Reed were huddled around a computer terminal in the library, arguing about how to spell *imbecile* and whether it looked better to print *D-W-I-G-H-T* across the top of the paper or down the left side, followed by the words *Dishonorable, Wormy, Insolent, Grievous, Harassing* and *Tormentor.*

Ms. Davidson, the librarian, caught sight of them. Sure they were up to no good, and in a hurry to finish cleaning the library by the end of the school day, she called Reed over to her office.

She was looking at the rabbit cage.

"I need you to carry the bunny to my car, Reed. I'm taking him home for summer vacation. Ooh"— she wrinkled her nose—"I guess his cage hasn't been cleaned out for a while. Be a dear and remove the soiled newspapers and replace them with a clean, dry lining, will you? There are plastic trash bags behind my desk. Be sure to dispose of the waste properly."

"Sure thing," Reed said, more enthusiastically than Miss Davidson would have expected. A few minutes later, after a whispered conference with Riley and Henry, he hurried out of the library with a plastic bag of rabbit turds.

Henry stood by the copier, scooping copies off the tray and keeping an eye on Riley, who had just accessed the entire school's email address book and sent a mass mailing (after double-checking the spelling of the phrases *barbarous imbecile*, *menacing tyrant* and *puerile brute*, as well as providing a hyperlink to his blog). Riley logged off, grabbed a roll of tape from Miss Davidson's desk and met Henry at the door.

By the time the next bell rang, 300 flyers had been taped on hallway walls or slid into faculty mailboxes and a bag of rabbit by-product had been smushed into the innersoles of the $350 gym shoes that rested in the backpack of one Dwight Hauser.

The three boys looked at their handiwork, high-fived and headed for the principal's office to turn themselves in. They might have been wrong in becoming vigilantes, but they weren't going to try to escape the blame.

"Well, men," Henry said, "it's been a pleasure and a privilege to redress an injustice with you. The flyers have flown, the emails have mailed and we have shown Dwight for the petty lowlife that he is. That was awesome, Riley, that you had snapped that picture of his hairy butt crack when he bent over in the locker room and that you cut and pasted it to the email. And Reed, that was a brilliant touch to put the bunny poop in his shoes—brings the whole thing full circle."

"It was," Riley agreed, "awesome."

"I'm so glad that someone other than me is going to wind up smelling like crap," Reed said.

"I can't wait for summer vacation," Henry said. "We've really been held back with the whole school thing. Imagine: three months of free time. And just as we're hitting our stride. People will read about us someday, songs will be sung and movies will be made celebrating Our Audacious Exploits. You watch."

Epilogue

"Men, I have a great idea," Henry said to Reed and Riley as they sat in the principal's office waiting for their parents. They'd been suspended with forty-seven minutes left in the school year and a wink and a handshake from the principal, who pretended to look stern.

"No!" Reed said sharply.

Henry jumped. "Okay, okay, I hear you."

"No more ideas," Reed continued, "until I figure out how to explain to my parents that I've been suspended for the last forty-seven minutes of school because of your last idea."

Riley didn't say anything, but he edged away from Henry on the bench.

Henry just smiled.

Henry's smile was one Reed and Riley had seen many times before—a smile of confidence and of knowledge that somehow, in some way, everything would work out all right.

When Reed and Riley saw Henry smile, they knew.

They knew that they would do whatever Henry's plan called for. They knew, furthermore, that they would *always* do whatever Henry's plan called for because, in the end, Henry had the best ideas, and his smile and his belief in his plans were so amazingly convincing.

But Reed knew one more thing: No matter what, he would never land in poop again.

And Riley knew, from the look on Marci Robbins's face when she poked her head into the principal's office and waved to him, clutching one of their flyers, that their exploits were finally going to Attract the Attention of Females.

About the Author

Gary Paulsen is the distinguished author of many critically acclaimed books for young people, including three Newbery Honor Books: *The Winter Room*, *Hatchet*, and *Dogsong*. He is the recipient of the Margaret A. Edwards Award for lifetime achievement in young adult literature. Among his Random House books are *Lawn Boy Returns*; *Woods Runner*; *Notes from the Dog*; *Mudshark*; *Lawn Boy*; *The Legend of Bass Reeves*; *The Amazing Life of Birds*; *The Time Hackers*; *Molly McGinty Has a Really Good Day*; *The Quilt* (a companion to *Alida's Song* and *The Cookcamp*); *The Glass Café*; *How Angel Peterson Got His Name*; *Guts: The True Stories Behind* Hatchet *and the Brian Books*; *The Beet Fields*; *Soldier's Heart*; *Brian's Return*, *Brian's Winter*, and *Brian's Hunt* (companions to *Hatchet*); *Father Water, Mother Woods*; and five books about Francis Tucket's adventures in the Old West. Gary Paulsen has also published fiction and nonfiction for adults, as well as picture books illustrated by his wife, the painter Ruth Wright Paulsen. Their most recent book is *Canoe Days*. The Paulsens live in Alaska, in New Mexico, and on the Pacific Ocean.

You can visit Gary Paulsen on the Web
at GaryPaulsen.com.